CW00958132

BBC

DOCTOR WHO

TIME TRAVELLER'S DIARY

BBC CHILDREN'S BOOKS

UK | USA | Canada | Ireland | Australia
India | New Zealand | South Africa

BBC Children's Books are published by Puffin Books,
part of the Penguin Random House group of companies
whose addresses can be found at global.penguinrandomhouse.com.

www.penguin.co.uk
www.puffin.co.uk
www.ladybird.co.uk

Penguin
Random House
UK

First published 2020
001

Text by Chris Farnell

A CIP catalogue record for this book is available from the British Library

ISBN: 978–1–405–94086–3

All correspondence to:
BBC Children's Books
Penguin Random House Children's
80 Strand, London WC2R 0RL

MIX
Paper from
responsible sources
FSC® C018179

Penguin Random House is committed to a
sustainable future for our business, our readers
and our planet. This book is made from Forest
Stewardship Council® certified paper.

BBC

DOCTOR WHO

TIME TRAVELLER'S DIARY

PUFFIN

A NOTE TO
WHOEVER FINDS THIS

You know, at times like this, when I'm hiding from a cybernetic velociraptor in the cargo hold of an alien spaceship flying over France, I'm reminded that time travel can be very confusing. Even before you get into fixed points, the Web of Time and people using words like 'wimey', hopping between the past, present and future can really fry your brain. Now, some species are adapted to this kind of living. Time Lords, for instance, tend to get fidgety if they have to live longer than a week in the right temporal order (Are Time Lords still around? It gets hard to keep track . . .)

But for us mere humans, time travel is like starting to read a book in the middle and then skipping forward and back through the pages. You might be able to guess the overall plot, but it quickly gets confusing.

That's why you need a diary. If time travel is like flicking through a book, this is your bookmark. It has served me well over the years and I've made a number of notes in it regarding events like holidays, places to visit and, well, places to avoid.

Hopefully, when I throw this out of the ship in a minute it will find its way to an adventurer who can make use of my notes. And there's plenty of room to add your own – when a time machine isn't available, a diary is the best method to get a message to your future self. Also, if at some point you pop by the invisible flying saucer above Carcassonne on 17 February 1283 at two o'clock in the afternoon, I'd appreciate it if you could bring some tranquiliser darts and a really big butterfly net.

Yours hopefully,

A fellow traveller

ALL ABOUT ME

Name:

Known aliases:

Address:

Home planet:

Species:

Picture:

PLACE
PHOTO
HERE

Number of hearts:

Colour of eyes:

Hair colour:

In case of emergency please contact:

Known allergies:

Languages spoken:

Special talents:

JANUARY 1st

New Year's Day on Planet Earth. Several New Year's Days in a row on Planet Apalapucia, depending on the timestream.

....

....

....

....

....

JANUARY 2nd

Bank holiday in Scotland, Earth. In 4196, employees at the Bank of Karabraxos were given their first – and last – day off.

....

....

....

....

....

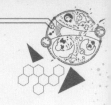

January 3rd

Across the Adipose nursery worlds, birth rates skyrocket as host species try to stick to their New Year's resolutions to lose weight.

....

....

....

....

....

January 4th

Observation of the Rites of the Tin Vagabond in the Metallarch System.

....

....

....

....

....

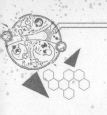

January 5th

On this day in 1972, President of the United States Richard Nixon ordered the building of a space shuttle. He was cagey when asked why, saying 'You don't know who might be listening . . .'

....

....

....

....

....

January 6th

The first day of the great Star Whale migration.

....

....

....

....

....

JANUARY 7th

In 1610, Galileo Galilei wrote in a letter that he had spotted three of Jupiter's moons. A few months later, he discovered a fourth. Humans had to wait until the twenty-ninth century to discover the final moon – the golden planet Voga.

....

....

....

....

JANUARY 8th

Elvis Presley was born on 8 January 1935. His lesser-known songs include 'Blue Suede Time Machine', 'Viva Las Vega' and 'Suspicious Mind-Reading Aliens'.

....

....

....

....

JANUARY 9th

Earth scientists announced the discovery of planets outside their solar system on 9 January 1992.
Planets outside their solar system had already discovered Earth.

....

....

....

....

....

JANUARY 10th

At their annual meeting in 2540, the Historical Monuments Preservation Society discussed plans to preserve
the Millennium Dome, the International Space Station and Jupiter's Great Red Spot,
which was originally due to disappear in 2039.

....

....

....

....

....

January 11th

The Dagmar Cluster hosted the great spaceship race in the fifty-first century.
If attending, beware ion storms and cannibal spaceships.

....

....

....

....

January 12th

In 1998, nineteen European countries agreed to ban human cloning. One hundred and
fifty years later the laws were expanded to include Gangers (Flesh duplicates).

....

....

....

....

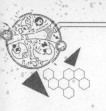

JANUARY 13th

Annual Slitheen family reunion.

....

....

....

....

....

JANUARY 14th

The Ogrons invaded Tivoli in 2064 and freed the planet from the Hath. They were welcomed as heroes.

....

....

....

....

....

JANUARY 15th

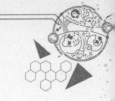

The Daleks celebrate Extermination Day. Also celebrated every other day in the Dalek calendar.

JANUARY 16th

In 1909 Ernest Shackleton's expedition fell just short of reaching the South Pole and therefore failed to notice the pair of Krynoid seedpods that had crashed there.

JANUARY 17th

Annual Organ Donor Awareness Dinner hosted by Harmony Shoal. Organ donations not optional.

....

....

....

....

JANUARY 18th

The date of the annual Space–Time Police Officers' Ball. The crew of the Teselecta, the Atraxi and the Shadow Proclamation meet to eat some vol-au-vents and share stories of their greatest arrests.

....

....

....

....

....

JANUARY 19th

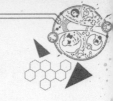

The birthdate of Edgar Allan Poe in 1809. Also the date the batteries are changed
in the ravens at the Tower of London each year.

....

....

....

....

JANUARY 20th

United States presidential inaugurations to see on this date include:
John F. Kennedy, the first Catholic president, in 1961.
Barack Obama, the first African-American president, in 2009.
Gavin A32X40, the first robot president, in 2086.

....

....

....

....

....

JANUARY 21st

NASA's Mars rover Spirit temporarily lost communication with Earth for two days in 2004 due to problems with the computer's memory . . . or Ice Warrior interference.

....

....

....

....

....

JANUARY 22nd

In 871, Vikings defeated an army of Saxons led by King Æthelred I in Hampshire. Before the battle, a mysterious figure dressed as a monk was seen trying to sell Æthelred used stun blasters.

....

....

....

....

....

January 23rd

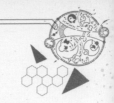

The Rock & Roll Hall of Fame inducted its first members in 1986, including Chuck Berry and James Brown. Subsequent inductees have included Aretha Franklin, David Bowie, Billie Eilish and Clone 9XZ3.

....

....

....

....

January 24th

Balhoonians, Crespallions, Stenza, Hooloovoo and other species of ultramarine skin colour joyfully celebrate Blue Monday. (NB Not always on a Monday.)

....

....

....

....

....

January 25th

Earth observes Burns Night to celebrate the Scottish poet Robert Burns.
Coincidentally, Pyrovillia observes Burns Night to celebrate burning things.

....

....

....

....

....

January 26th

On this day in 2020 the VOR search engine and social media site undergoes a massive software update,
making it 50% more secure against extra-dimensional alien invasions.

....

....

....

....

....

January 27th

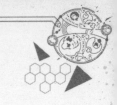

Earth's nations signed the Outer Space Treaty in 1967,
which limited the use of the Moon and other celestial bodies to peaceful exploration.

···

···

···

···

January 28th

The Silurians and Sea Devils signed a peace deal in 425 million BC.

···

···

···

···

···

JANUARY 29th

Every year on this day, many humans complain that January seems longer than other months.
Possibly the result of temporal distortion.

....

....

....

....

....

JANUARY 30th

The beginning of the largest and most spectacular sporting event in the entire universe,
the Ultra Bowl. Has an ad break that lasts approximately two and a half weeks.

....

....

....

....

....

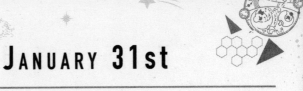

JANUARY 31st

Deadline to submit intergalactic tax returns to the Shadow Proclamation.
Enforced by crack squadrons of Judoon accountants.

....

....

....

....

FEBRUARY 1st

In 2007 on Parallel Earth, the President of Great Britain was assassinated by Cybermen.

....

....

....

....

....

FEBRUARY **2nd**

Time loops are common around this date.

....

....

....

....

....

FEBRUARY **3rd**

Sontaran Day of Remembrance, when Sontarans remember their favourite wars.

....

....

....

....

....

February 4th

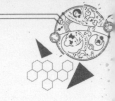

A frost fair was held in London on 4 February 1814. Attendees included humans . . . and the monster that lived under the ice of the frozen Thames.

....

....

....

....

February 5th

The Ellarchon Dyson Sphere collapsed in 8891.

....

....

....

....

FEBRUARY 6th

Millennial celebration of the Festival of Offerings on Tiaanamat, Akhaten.
If attending do not, under any circumstances, interrupt the singing.

....

....

....

....

....

FEBRUARY 7th

In 850,000 BC somebody walked across some mud in Happisburgh, Norfolk. The discovery of their footprints
was reported on exactly 852,014 years later, when scientists declared them to be the oldest footprints by
early humans ever found outside of Africa. If visiting, don't wear trainers.

....

....

....

....

....

FEBRUARY 8th

Shakri Festival of Giving. Do not accept the small black cubes on offer.

FEBRUARY 9th

The Great Meteor Procession occurred in 1913. It may have been a small, short-lived moon breaking up in the Earth's atmosphere or a failed alien invasion.

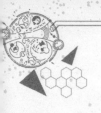

FEBRUARY 10th

The wedding of Queen Victoria and Prince Albert took place in 1840.

....

....

....

....

FEBRUARY 11th

The annual All-Planets Championship Mechboxing Tournament.
Beware of ringside seats as they are within blast radius.

....

....

....

....

....

FEBRUARY 12th

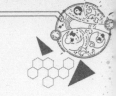

Lady Jane Grey, otherwise known as the 'Nine Days' Queen', was executed in 1554. It was the shortest reign of a British monarch until Queen Liz IV's coronation space yacht passed through the Time Vortex. Her entire reign lasted thirty-six minutes.

FEBRUARY 13th

In 2174, the Uvodni seized Tivoli and liberated it from the Ogrons. They were welcomed as heroes.

FEBRUARY **14th**

Great Valentine's Day hotspots of the universe include:

The Singing Towers of Darillium

The Asgardian picnic ground

Paris

....

....

....

....

....

FEBRUARY **15th**

Event One: the Big Bang (the birth of the universe) occurred on this date in the year 13,500,017,903 BC at 11 a.m. Travel to a time before this date is inadvisable.

....

....

....

....

....

FEBRUARY 16th

In the year 4.8/Pomegranate/12 the Church of the Meme splits into two religious sects- the Adherence to the Repeated Meme and the Subversion of the Repeated Meme.

FEBRUARY 17th

The Teeth Gathering of Calciarnus VI.

FEBRUARY 18th

Pluto was discovered in 1930. In August 2006 astronomers reclassified it as a dwarf planet.

....

....

....

....

....

FEBRUARY 19th

Date of the annual neighbourhood-watch meeting in Trap Street, London.
If attending, a human guise is required.

....

....

....

....

....

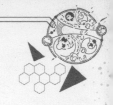

FEBRUARY 20th

The Silurian Palaeontology Society opened their exhibition 'When Mammals Walked the Earth' in 3065.

....

....

....

....

....

FEBRUARY 21st

The date of the annual Zygon Celebrity-Lookalike Competition. Competitors must bring their own celebrities.

....

....

....

....

....

FEBRUARY 22nd

The shade artists of Adumbratia VI attempted to put on a shadow-puppet show with trained Vashta Nerada, but the premiere ended in disaster when there was a power cut.

....

....

....

....

....

FEBRUARY 23rd

The Miniscope Prohibition Treaty was signed in 2172.

....

....

....

....

....

February 24th

The date of the final Mr Universe competition in 7429, when Mr Universe –
a small, sentient universe – was declared the conclusive winner.

....

....

....

....

February 25th

The Battle of the Nine Suns was waged in 4136.

....

....

....

....

....

FEBRUARY 26th

The first* official contact between humans and an extraterrestrial intelligence occurred in 2085.
*Excluding alien invasions, alien refugees living in disguise on Earth,
aliens secretly guiding human evolution throughout history and tourists.

....

....

....

....

FEBRUARY 27th

In 2032, a computer beat the reigning world champion at charades for the first time.

....

....

....

....

....

FEBRUARY 28th

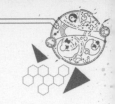

In 1939, Earth was invaded by the Dord, a species of brain parasite that transport themselves through language. Fortunately the invasion was limited to a single dictionary.

FEBRUARY 29th

Annual parade of the Church of the Silence. (Does not take place on leap years.)
The most unforgettable party that you'll never remember attending.

MARCH 1st

St David's Day. A good time to absorb rift energy in scenic Cardiff.

....

....

....

....

....

MARCH 2nd

In 1996, a café in Grantham sold the best fry-up ever made. Arrive early to avoid crowds of
time travellers who flock to the time and place of the legendary breakfast.

....

....

....

....

....

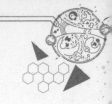

MARCH **3rd**

World Wildlife Day on Earth. Expanded to Worlds Wildlife Day in 2115.

....

....

....

....

MARCH **4th**

Sontar's very first Give Peace a Chance Day in 4001. The Sontarans gave peace a chance.
They didn't like it.

....

....

....

....

March 5th

In 2005, London was invaded by the Nestene Consciousness using an army of Autons posing as shop-window mannequins.

....

....

....

....

....

March 6th

In 7100 the Teselecta court began hearings for the case The People v Every Evil Figure in History.

....

....

....

....

....

MARCH 7th

The Kaldoran Robot Union was founded in 3030.

....

....

....

....

....

MARCH 8th

International Women's Day on Earth. Expanded to Interstellar Women's Day in 2115.

....

....

....

....

....

MARCH 9th

The Vogan Gold Rush began in 2877.

....

....

....

....

....

MARCH 10th

Alexander Graham Bell made the first – ever telephone call in 1876.

....

....

....

....

....

March 11th

Cryogenic Suspension Day took place in 2651. Cryogenic Awakening Day took place in 3651.

....

....

....

....

March 12th

1,000 zettabytes of classified data was stolen from the Darkstar archives by DNA smugglers in 6980.

....

....

....

....

....

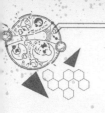

March 13th

The first day of the Rally of the Twelve Galaxies. Four thousand contestants start out on a race that will take them across 209 terrains and ninety-four planets. Only one will win the 3.2 trillion krin prize.

....

....

....

....

March 14th

Pi Day, so called because the date looks like the ratio of the circumference of a circle to its diameter: 3.14. As pi actually has infinite digits, true Pi Day can only be found on planets with a far more complex calendar.

....

....

....

....

....

MARCH 15th

Julius Caesar was assassinated in 44 BC. Fixed point in time — do not interfere.

....

....

....

....

....

MARCH 16th

The Lux Foundation Library — a planet-sized collection of every book in existence — was quarantined in 5050 when 4,022 visitors went missing. Return all books by this date.

....

....

....

....

....

MARCH 17th

St Patrick's Day celebrated in Ireland.
(Which is not, despite what some Earthlings believe, the home of Gallifrey.)

....

....

....

....

....

MARCH 18th

The Voord conquered Tivoli in 2293 and overthrew the Uvodni. They were welcomed as heroes.

....

....

....

....

....

March 19th

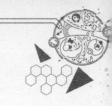

The asteroid of Demon's Run was reopened as a museum in 5168.

....

....

....

....

March 20th

International Day of Happiness. Avoid Vardy-constructed colonies on this date,
as the robots sometimes enforce the day with deadly efficiency.

....

....

....

....

MARCH 21st

International Day of Forests. Not to be confused with the Day of the International Forest, when the Earth was covered in a single forest to ward off a solar flare.

....

....

....

....

....

MARCH 22nd

World Water Day. Be careful drinking water on new worlds as it may be poisonous . . . or sentient.

....

....

....

....

....

MARCH 23rd

In 2010, a pioneering scientist among the Boneless raised the idea of a hypothetical third dimension.

....

....

....

....

MARCH 24th

The Yggdrasilians draw the sap of the planetary World Tree on this date each year.

....

....

....

....

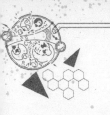

MARCH 25th

The Space Hindenburg crashed in 4386. In the aftermath of the disaster, a law was passed banning manufacturers from naming starships after historic craft without first reading at least one book about them.

....

....

....

....

....

MARCH 26th

On this date in 1455 the last-ever chair was manufactured on Skaro.

....

....

....

....

....

MARCH 27th

Chelonians make the annual migration back to their home world to lay their eggs.

....

....

....

....

....

MARCH 28th

In 2276, Earth's space fleets finally switched from using 'red alert' to using 'mauve alert' in line with the rest of the universe.

....

....

....

....

....

MARCH 29th

In 1974, the Terracotta Army was discovered in Shaanxi province, China. Five hundred years later the Silver Army was discovered on the planet Telos with disastrous results.

....

....

....

....

MARCH 30th

Thousands died in a mass spectrox leak on Androzani Minor in 5110.

....

....

....

....

....

March **31st**

The first sentient computer virus was born in 2099.

April **1st**

April Fool's Day. On average only half of the alien sightings reported on this day are true.

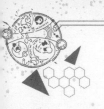

APRIL 2nd

The uncoronation of the Could've Been King was held in 199312.

....

....

....

....

....

APRIL 3rd

The season finale of Bear With Me, a reality television show about six contestants who live with a bear in a small space station, aired on 3 April 200098. It was the most-watched television episode in the Third Quadrant of the galaxy.

....

....

....

....

....

April 4th

The Stenza captured Tivoli in 2304 and wiped out the Voord. They were welcomed as heroes.

....

....

....

....

....

April 5th

In 2034, the Wire briefly conquered Earth after someone accidentally posted it
on the internet as a video and it went viral.

....

....

....

....

....

APRIL 6th

Bring a Human to Work Day at Kerblam head office on the moon of Kandoka.

....

....

....

....

....

APRIL 7th

On this day at the dawn of the universe, the first act of vandalism occurred: a cliff face on Planet One was defaced. Academics have spent millennia debating the meaning of the graffiti.

....

....

....

....

....

APRIL 8th

In 1969 a police telephone box appeared out of nowhere in the Oval Office at the White House. Nobody can remember why.

....

....

....

....

....

APRIL 9th

The colony of Phantasmagoria VII was overrun by a wave of Gelth hauntings in 3113.

....

....

....

....

....

APRIL 10th

The lost moon of Poosh reappeared in 5999, ruining the careers of academics
who'd spent their lives looking for it.

....

....

....

....

....

APRIL 11th

The human—Zarbi wars came to an end in 4530, when Earth faced an insect-repellent shortage.

....

....

....

....

....

APRIL 12th

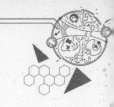

The first manned spaceflight *was performed by Yuri Gagarin in 1961.
* *Not counting time travellers, alien abductions, Victorians stealing crashed Martian technology or any employee, member or affiliate of the Torchwood Institute.*

....

....

....

....

APRIL 13th

In 7710, Lord Power began his reign as the head of the Third Great and Bountiful Human Empire.

....

....

....

....

....

APRIL **14th**

The Hotel Madame du Barry was closed down in 5026 after the hotel AI tried to fix a plumbing problem by using the guests as spare parts.

....

....

....

....

APRIL **15th**

The Upgrade Wars began in 2342, when two factions of Cybermen couldn't agree on which operating system to use.

....

....

....

....

....

APRIL **16th**

Rejarring Day on Skaro. Infant Dalek mutants are moved to bigger jars to accommodate their growth cycle.

....

....

....

....

APRIL **17th**

In 1970, Apollo 13 safely returned to Earth after an oxygen tank exploded and created a shortage of heat, power and water, which forced the crew to carry out ingenious makeshift repairs.

....

....

....

....

....

APRIL **18th**

In 3760 activists formed a movement, known as the Slumber Party, to ban the Morpheus pods responsible for the Triton Sandman outbreak.

....

....

....

....

....

APRIL **19th**

In 1971, Earth launched its first space station, Salyut 1. Unlike future Earth space stations, Salyut 1 did not have artificial gravity, any good restaurants or its own TV studio.

....

....

....

....

....

APRIL 20th

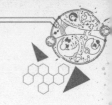

The Time Vortex experiences high volumes of traffic and frequent paradox clusters around this date.

....

....

....

....

APRIL 21st

Queen Elizabeth II of the United Kingdom, Earth, famous for staying in Buckingham Palace through multiple alien invasions, was born on 21 April 1926.

....

....

....

....

....

APRIL 22nd

The Time Lord known as the Doctor died at Lake Silencio in 2011. This is a fixed point in time and there is no chance the Doctor survived. Any reports of the Doctor existing after this point are the result of an overactive imagination.

....

....

....

....

APRIL 23rd

William Shakespeare was born on 23 April 1564. He is credited with the invention of over 1,700 words, although later scholars believe some of them originated on alien planets.

....

....

....

....

....

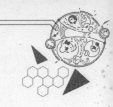

APRIL 24th

The Androgum Dinner Wars ended in 2240 with the Dessert Treaty.

....

....

....

....

....

APRIL 25th

DNA Day on Earth commemorates the discovery of the structure of DNA by Rosalind Franklin, Maurice Wilkins, Francis Crick and James Watson on this day in 1953. Do not edit your own DNA at home.

....

....

....

....

....

APRIL 26th

Logopolitan number farmers faced a dangerous famine following an outbreak of minuses in 3250.

....

....

....

....

APRIL 27th

One of Vincent van Gogh's last paintings, Blue Box Exploding, was stolen from the
National Gallery on Starship UK in 5145.

....

....

....

....

....

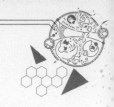

APRIL 28th

Start of the rainy season in Saturn's northern hemisphere. The rain is made of diamonds, so pack a strong umbrella and a bucket if you're visiting.

....

....

....

....

....

APRIL 29th

Earth celebrates International Dance Day. Popular dances in the twelve galaxies include the waltz, the bolero, the six-legged two-step, the eight-dimensional tango and the drunk giraffe.

....

....

....

....

....

APRIL 30th

The Gaelic festival Beltane begins at midnight – in the first minute of the first day of May.
Beware possible incursions from Dæmons on this date.

....

....

....

....

MAY 1st

The Empire State Building opened in 1931 (despite Dalek interference).

....

....

....

....

....

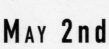
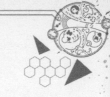

MAY 2nd

The ancient Lost City of Leicester was discovered in 11529.

....

....

....

....

MAY 3rd

The Johannesburg Space Elevator collapsed in 2089.

....

....

....

....

....

MAY 4th

The Doom Moon of the Sixth Great and Bountiful Human Empire was destroyed in 7791.

....

....

....

....

....

MAY 5th

Transmat Splicing Awareness Day.

....

....

....

....

....

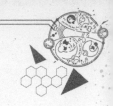

MAY 6th

The last-known Wirrn egg was stolen in 17000. Current whereabouts unknown.

....

....

....

....

MAY 7th

The crew of the Fancy mutinied when the feared pirate Captain Henry Avery took command in 1694. The fate of the ship is unknown, but over the following centuries several alien species reported sightings of its crew.

....

....

....

....

....

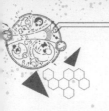

MAY 8th

VE (Victory in Europe) Day, marking the Allied victory in Europe on 8 May 1945 during World War II.

....

....

....

....

....

MAY 9th

VE (Victory on Earth) Day, marking the victory of human resistance fighters
on 9 May 2164 against the Dalek invasion of Earth.

....

....

....

....

....

MAY 10th

VEE (Victory on Epsilon Eridani) Day, marking the victory of Epsilon Eridanians on 10 May 2470 against human occupiers.

....

....

....

....

....

MAY 11th

Using Bliss patches is banned on New Venus in 4999999974.

....

....

....

....

....

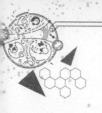

MAY 12th

The first day of the Krynoid growth season.

....

....

....

....

....

MAY 13th

Ux Census Day on Ranskoor Av Kolos. As the species only ever has two living members, the census takes approximately eight seconds to complete.

....

....

....

....

....

MAY **14th**

The eclipse of the Vashta Nerada on Solon IX occurred in 5090.
Onlookers were thrilled until they realised Solon IX didn't have a moon.

....

....

....

....

MAY **15th**

Las Vegas was founded in 1905. Space Vegas was founded in 3005. As well as money, the casinos of Space
Vegas accept luck, days of your future, memories and hope as currency.

....

....

....

....

....

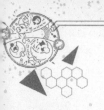

MAY 16th

The Covenant of the Pandorica was signed in various time zones.

....

....

....

....

....

MAY 17th

The date of the annual Nimon Porcelain Fair.

....

....

....

....

....

MAY 18th

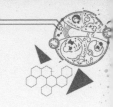

International Museum Day. Offers a way for time travellers to find lost property or new places to visit and, sometimes, to keep score. Popular museums include the Solarian Pinacotheque, the Delirium Archive, the Eldred Collection, Henry van Statten's vault, the Space Museum and the Time Museum.

....

....

....

....

MAY 19th

The Raxacoricofallapatorians annexed Tivoli in 2311,
stealing it from the Stenza. They were welcomed as heroes.

....

....

....

....

MAY 20th

In 3808, Ganymede Systems launched their 'two breaths for the price of one!'
sale across the outer solar system.

....

....

....

....

....

MAY 21th

The first day of the Malmooth laying season.

....

....

....

....

....

MAY 22nd

Earth's first colony on Mars, Bowie Base One, celebrated its first successful potato crop in 2069.

....

....

....

....

....

MAY 23rd

World Turtle Day. Not to be confused with Turtle World Day,
which marks the first contact between humans and Chelonians.

....

....

....

....

....

MAY 24th

In 9100 Reapers swarmed through the Bootstrap Expanse.

....

....

....

....

....

MAY 25th

The SpaceX Dragon became the first commercial spacecraft to rendezvous with
Earth's International Space Station in 2012.

....

....

....

....

....

MAY 26th

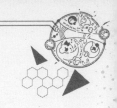

In 2210 the population of Driax V were certain they had been overrun by a Kantrofarri (dream crab) infestation. The invasion was revealed to be a dream, brought on by a Kantrofarri infestation.

....

....

....

....

....

MAY 27th

The date of the annual Skithra Science Fair, when the greatest robotic scorpion scientists meet to show off their latest stolen inventions.

....

....

....

....

....

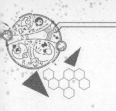

MAY 28th

The Delta III Calamari Banquet took place in 5123.

....

....

....

....

MAY 29th

UNIT was founded in the 1970s . . . or possibly the 1980s.

....

....

....

....

....

MAY 30th

The first day of the Nestene plastic-harvesting season.

....

....

....

....

MAY 31th

The RMS Titanic was launched in 1911. Do not book a ticket on this or the
Max Capricorn space cruise liner of the same name.

....

....

....

....

....

JUNE 1st

The annual general election of Colony Sarff.

....

....

....

....

JUNE 2nd

The coronation of Queen Elizabeth II took place on this day in 1953.

....

....

....

....

....

June 3rd

Second Cousin of Mine, of the Family of Blood, was arrested on this day 50236 while trying to steal medical Nanogenes from a life-extension clinic.

....

....

....

....

....

June 4th

The Silurian Ark was launched in 100 million BC.

....

....

....

....

....

June 5th

The first journey of the Orient Express took place in 1883.
The first journey of the Space Orient Express took place in 4355.

....

....

....

....

....

June 6th

The Atraxi extradimensional prison break occurred in 2009.

....

....

....

....

....

June 7th

The last-ever Mondasian Olympics was held in 1984
after all the Cybermen competitors drew in every single event.

....

....

....

....

June 8th

At 10 a.m. on 8 June 6492, the Great Hoppledomian Fruit Fly War broke out on Hoppledom VI.
The war would last for fifty generations, concluding at 3.30 p.m. that afternoon.

....

....

....

....

....

JUNE 9th

The Minister of War rose to power and their reign of ultimate terror began on this day in 2030.

....

....

....

....

JUNE 10th

In 1816, Lord Byron, Percy Shelley, Mary Godwin, Doctor John Polidori and Claire Clairmont stayed at Villa Diodati, Lake Geneva. Over three rainy days, as part of a competition to see who could write the scariest story, Mary Godwin wrote 'Frankenstein', a story about a monster made of human parts.
For centuries people have wondered where she got her idea . . .

....

....

....

....

....

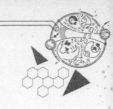

June 11th

In 2022, you dropped your breakfast and the toast landed butter-side down.
This is a fixed point in time. Do not attempt to avert it or you could destroy the universe.

....

....

....

....

....

June 12th

The first day of Nimon faith-harvesting season.

....

....

....

....

....

JUNE 13th

Pioneer 10 became the first man-made object to leave the central solar system
when it flew past the orbit of Neptune on this day in 1983.

....

....

....

....

....

JUNE 14th

The Judoon placed Tivoli under their jurisdiction in 2426 and
arrested the Raxacoricofallapatorians. They were welcomed as heroes.

....

....

....

....

....

JUNE 15th

The Magna Carta was signed in 1215 . . . in spite of possible alien interference.

....

....

....

....

JUNE 16th

Every 200 years, the planet Brigadoonicon VII shifts into phase with normal time for twenty-four hours.

....

....

....

....

....

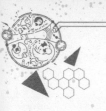

June 17th

The first session of the Kahler war crimes tribunal was held in 1860.

....

....

....

....

....

June 18th

In 1178, five medieval monks in Canterbury Earth saw 'a flaming torch' spring out of the Moon, spewing 'fire, hot coals and sparks'. Scientists used to think this was the collision that created the Giordano Bruno crater, although by the mid-21st century most scientists agree it was the Moon beginning to hatch.

....

....

....

....

....

JUNE 19th

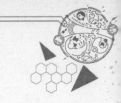

Chronovore Paradox Yield Day.

....

....

....

....

JUNE 20th

The date of the annual leadership lottery on Gamblax IV.

....

....

....

....

....

JUNE 21st

A Tritovore trade caravan crashed at San Helios in 2009.

....

....

....

....

....

JUNE 22nd

In 4331, the first verse of 'Ood Star Requiem, a song that lasted for 10,000 years, began.

....

....

....

....

....

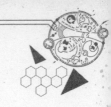

June 23rd

UNIT was disbanded in 2019. Great place and time to pick up forbidden alien artefacts on the cheap.

....

....

....

....

....

June 24th

Take Your Dog to Work Day. Includes robotic dogs Cybershades and Stigorax.

....

....

....

....

....

June 25th

Mondasian Christmas.

....

....

....

....

....

June 26th

According to the Institute of Temporal Consistency, deep scans of the tissue of space–time
indicate the entire universe – past, present and future – exploded on this day in 2010.
This has left a lot of scientists very confused about why we still exist.

....

....

....

....

....

JUNE 27th

Salt-Awareness Day on Jaconda.

....

....

....

....

JUNE 28th

In 2009 famed scientist Stephen Hawking held a party for time travellers at
Gonville & Caius College, Cambridge, but he only sent out invites after the event.

....

....

....

....

JUNE 29th

The last day of the Luna University spring semester.

....

....

....

....

....

JUNE 30th

The Tunguska event occurred on Earth in 1908. A mysterious explosion – possibly an asteroid impact or a spaceship crash – flattened 2,000 square kilometres of Siberian forest.

....

....

....

....

....

JULY 1st

King Hydroflax's reheading ceremony took place in the fifty-fourth century.

··

··

··

··

JULY 2nd

World UFO Day on Earth.

··

··

··

··

··

JULY 3rd

Vervoid Vote-o-synthesis Day.

....

....

....

....

....

JULY 4th

Declarations of independence made on this date include:
United States, Earth, 1776
Mars, 2130
New United States, New Earth, 5000000076

....

....

....

....

....

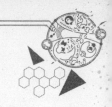

JULY 5th

Isaac Newton published Philosophiæ Naturalis Principia Mathematica in 1687, which explained his theory of gravity.

....

....

....

....

JULY 6th

The date of the ascension of the Ice Warrior Empress of Mars in 3000 BC.

....

....

....

....

....

JULY 7th

The first day of the Nanogene spore cycle.

....

....

....

....

....

JULY 8th

In 1947, something – believed to be an alien spacecraft – crashed in Roswell, New Mexico.

....

....

....

....

....

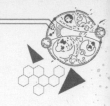

July 9th

The Kraal marched into Tivoli in 2559 and usurped the Judoon. They were welcomed as heroes.

....

....

....

....

July 10th

The Eighth Great and Bountiful Human Empire fell to the Deathsmiths of Goth in 9967.

....

....

....

....

....

JULY 11th

Davros's birthday.

....

....

....

....

JULY 12th

Charles Babbage hosted a technological exhibition on this day in 1834, only for it to be disrupted by the appearance of a mysterious woman and a man with a shrinking device, who murdered several guests.

....

....

....

....

....

July **13th**

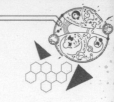

Skovox Blitzer Armistice declared in 2320.

....

....

....

....

July **14th**

Cleaning day took place at Paradise Towers in 2157. If attending, take weapons.

....

....

....

....

JULY 15th

The Rosetta Stone was discovered in 1799, giving archaeologists the ability to translate Ancient Egyptian hieroglyphics for first time. The Rosetta Stone II, carved 9,000 years later, was updated to include translations for Neo-Martian, Krop Tor script and Emoji.

....

....

....

....

JULY 16th

In 1966, the artificial superintelligence WOTAN failed to take over the Earth. It had attempted to do so by connecting all the computers on the planet together in a sort of worldwide web.

....

....

....

....

....

July 17th

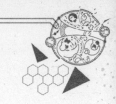

The Human–Hath War began on this day in 6012.

July 18th

The day of the Sense Sphere psychic election.

JULY **19th**

The Great Fire of Rome, Earth, began on this day in 64 AD.
The fire raged for nine days, destroying two thirds of the city.

....

....

....

....

....

JULY **20th**

Neil Armstrong became the first ('You should kill us all on sight!') human to walk on the Moon in 1969.

....

....

....

....

....

JULY 21st

The annual Androzani–Cheem tree fair. Ask permission before picking any fruit.

....

....

....

....

JULY 22nd

A second group of English colonists arrived at Roanoke Island in 1587 after the first group mysteriously disappeared, leaving only the word 'Croatoan' carved into a tree. No bodies were ever found.

....

....

....

....

....

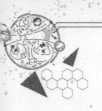

JULY 23rd

A three-week party that took place in Essex in 1138 saw the invention
of the word 'dude' and music played with an electric guitar.

....

....

....

....

....

JULY 24th

The Human—Hath War ended this day in 6012.

....

....

....

....

....

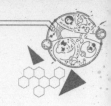

July 25th

The probe Viking 1 photographed the Cydonia region of Mars in 1976,
revealing a rock formation that looked eerily like a human face.

....

....

....

....

July 26th

The day the Cyberleader typically installs the latest software updates, removing bugs like 'mercy' and
adding further improvements to make the Cybermen more terrifying for users.

....

....

....

....

....

July **27th**

The opening ceremony for the London Olympic Games took place in 2012. After the original torchbearer stumbled and fell, the Olympic flame was rescued by a mysterious thin man in a suit.

....

....

....

....

....

July **28th**

The Halassi Androvar diamond was returned to its people in 5343.

....

....

....

....

....

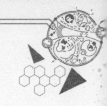

July 29th

The dancing plague spread through Strasbourg, Earth, in 1518. Victims were forced to dance for days without stopping and some even died from the affliction.

....

....

....

....

July 30th

The 'Touch the Spaceship' contest took place on Bad Wolf TV in 200118. The last person with a hand, tentacle or cybernetic prosthetic on the spaceship was declared the winner.

....

....

....

....

....

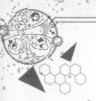

JULY 31st

Clone Batch Draining Day on the Sontaran home worlds.

....

....

....

....

AUGUST 1st

The first sandminers began operating on Kaldor in 2799.

....

....

....

....

....

August 2nd

The date of the biannual Dalek parliamentary elections.
So far they have unanimously voted for 'EXTERMINATE!' every time.

....

....

....

....

August 3rd

The Papal Mainframe was assassinated in 6972.

....

....

....

....

....

AUGUST **4th**

Summer holiday recommendation: the famous automatic sands of Space Florida in 2690.

....

....

....

....

AUGUST **5th**

Summer holiday recommendation: the Honey Moon .
Take care, as the honey may be sentient and a bit carnivorous.

....

....

....

....

....

AUGUST 6th

In 1996, scientists at NASA announced that they had found evidence of primitive organisms on the Martian asteroid ALH 84001.

....

....

....

....

AUGUST 7th

Summer holiday recommendation: the diamond planet of Midnight, which has a sapphire waterfall and an antigravity restaurant.

....

....

....

....

....

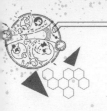

August 8th

The Great Train Robbery took place in 1963. The Great Starship Robbery took place in 4995.

....

....

....

....

....

August 9th

Summer holiday recommendation: the Argolin Leisure Hive.

....

....

....

....

....

AUGUST 10th

The Venusian Aikido Championship Finals.

....

....

....

....

....

AUGUST 11th

Summer holiday recommendation: the South Wales holiday camp Shangri-La in 1959.

....

....

....

....

....

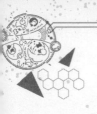

AUGUST 12th

The Terileptils occupied Tivoli in 2630 and kicked out the Kraal. They were welcomed as heroes.

....

....

....

....

AUGUST 13th

Summer holiday recommendation: Hedgewick's World of Wonders in 3498.

....

....

....

....

....

August 14th

The Thijarians witnessed the partition of India in 1947.

....

....

....

....

....

August 15th

King Macbeth of Scotland died in battle on 15 August 1057.
He may have been inspired by Carrionite prophecies.

....

....

....

....

....

AUGUST **16th**

Summer holiday recommendation: the Thrasymachus, a galaxy-class starliner touring the crystal worlds.

....

....

....

....

AUGUST **17th**

Summer holiday recommendation: cretaceous safari on Earth in 65.5 million BC.
Avoid treading on any butterflies.

....

....

....

....

....

AUGUST 18th

The last day of Woodstock in 1969. The music festival inspired the space colony Planet Woodstock, a world where the best musicians in the galaxy perform but there are no proper toilets.

....

....

....

....

....

AUGUST 19th

Witch trials were held on Earth in Samlesbury, England, in 1612, and in Salem, Massachusetts, USA, in 1692. None of the victims were witches, Carrionites or Morax.

....

....

....

....

....

August **20th**

Humans discovered the cure for Petrifold Regression in 5000001023.

....

....

....

....

....

August **21st**

National Radio Silence Day. In 1924 the United States Naval Observatory asked civilians to maintain radio silence for five minutes every hour to make it easier to detect radio signals from aliens.

....

....

....

....

....

AUGUST 22nd

The Battle of Bosworth took place on this day in 1485 in the country of England, Earth.
The remains of King Richard III, who died in the battle, were found beneath a car park in Leicester in 2012.

....

....

....

....

AUGUST 23rd

The Great Woolly Rebellion began in 2211.

....

....

....

....

....

AUGUST **24th**

Mount Vesuvius erupted on this day in 79 AD. Possibly caused by Pyrovile activity.
If visiting, don't buy anything off a man calling himself 'Captain Jack'.

....

....

....

....

AUGUST **25th**

A massive quantum waveform collapsed and created the Medusa Cascade 287 years after the Big Bang.

....

....

....

....

....

August **26th**

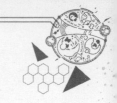

Krakatoa erupted on this day in 1883.

....

....

....

....

August **27th**

The art world was thrown into turmoil in 2100 when it was revealed that the Mona Lisa was a fake.

....

....

....

....

....

AUGUST 28th

The Memory Worm plague of Amnesiox IIX took place in an unknown year.

....

....

....

....

AUGUST 29th

Summer holiday recommendation: the Great City of the Exxilons,
one of the 700 Wonders of the Universe. (Closed due to Dalek activity in 2570.)

....

....

....

....

....

August **30th**

Summer holiday recommendation: Brighton.

....

....

....

....

August **31st**

The Face of Boe gave birth to a Boe-let in 200000. He named her Boemina.

....

....

....

....

....

SEPTEMBER 1st

In 1859 Earth experienced one of the biggest solar storms on record, the Carrington Event.
As Earth advanced technologically, it became increasingly vulnerable to these events.
Future storms caused widespread electrical blackouts and flesh-avatar autonomy.

....

....

....

....

....

SEPTEMBER 2nd

The Great Fire of London started at a Pudding Lane bakery in 1666.

....

....

....

....

....

SEPTEMBER 3rd

In 90000, the first human starship reached the edge of the observable universe, 47 billion light years away. They sent one hyperspace message: 'Oh my God, it's —', and were never heard from again.

....

....

....

....

....

SEPTEMBER 4th

Feline sapiens were recognised as a sentient species in 4500000025. Keeping them as pets was made illegal.

....

....

....

....

....

SEPTEMBER 5th

Earth launched the Voyager 1 probe in 1977. Onboard the craft was a gold-plated disc that contained images and recordings of Earth cultures, music, lifeforms and even human brain waves.
The aliens who found it reportedly said it was 'very funny'.

....

....

....

....

SEPTEMBER 6th

Term started for the Calvierri School in 1580. Take a pencil case, ruler and suntan lotion if you are attending.

....

....

....

....

SEPTEMBER 7th

The exodus of Doggerland occurred in 6200 BC. Stone Age peoples fled the land bridge connecting the British Isles to continental Europe. Possible Sea Devil involvement.

....

....

....

....

SEPTEMBER 8th

In 2016, the Osiris-Rex probe, the first probe sent to an asteroid to gather samples for Earth, was launched on its journey to the 101955 Bennu asteroid.

....

....

....

....

....

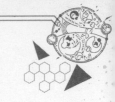

September 9th

The Vespiforms declared jam to be illegal in the Silfrax Galaxy in 2367.

....

....

....

....

September 10th

The Large Hadron Collider was turned on for the first time in 2008. Humans used the LHC, the biggest machine on Earth, to study the Higgs boson, a particle that gives mass to matter. Despite some fears, turning the LHC on didn't create a black hole that devoured the Earth.

....

....

....

....

....

SEPTEMBER 11th

The first cybernetic arms appeared in Mondasian shops in 1966.

....

....

....

....

SEPTEMBER 12th

Earth–Draconian Friendship Day.

....

....

....

....

....

SEPTEMBER 13th

In 1752 Earth's British Empire adopted the Gregorian calendar, skipping from 2 September to 14 September overnight. Nobody knows where the intervening eleven days went, but best not to set your time machine to this date to be on the safe side.

....

....

....

....

....

SEPTEMBER 14th

In 2015 human scientists observed gravitational waves for the first time, 150 years before the first gravity surfing tournament.

....

....

....

....

....

SEPTEMBER 15th

The HMS Beagle, with Charles Darwin aboard, reached the Galapagos Islands in 1835. The book this trip inspired, On the Origin of Species, changed the way humans thought about evolution. His other book, On the Origin of Alien Species, was never published.

....

....

....

....

SEPTEMBER 16th

Magnus Greel fled the Battle of Reykjavik in 5000, ending World War VI.

....

....

....

....

....

September 17th

The Vinvocci raided Tivoli in 2721 and exiled the Terileptils. They were welcomed as heroes.

....

....

....

....

September 18th

Eldrad of Kastria was sentenced to death in 150 million BC. He was cut into pieces and scattered across the universe.

....

....

....

....

SEPTEMBER 19th

Talk Like a Pirate Day.

....

....

....

....

SEPTEMBER 20th

Talk Like a Space Pirate Day.

....

....

....

....

....

SEPTEMBER 21st

On this day in 2360, from the top of a 400-foot-tall tree on Calderon Beta, more stars could be seen in the sky than at any other point in history.

....

....

....

....

....

SEPTEMBER 22nd

The 'Save the Human' campaign began in 57450, averting the extinction of the endangered species. Once hunting and eating humans was banned, the population recovered.

....

....

....

....

....

SEPTEMBER 23rd

The planet Neptune was discovered by humans in 1846.

SEPTEMBER 24th

Banned Books Week. Notable banned books include: The Sybilline Oracles, The True History of Planets, The Worshipful and Ancient Law of Gallifrey, The Book of the Still and River Song's diary.

SEPTEMBER 25th

The beginning of the Sycorax Bone Festival.

....

....

....

....

SEPTEMBER 26th

Albert Einstein published his special theory of relativity in 1905 and
paved the way for the first human time travellers.

....

....

....

....

....

SEPTEMBER **27th**

The harvest of the singing corn on Metadelphia VI.

....

....

....

....

SEPTEMBER **28th**

The first day of the Isolus migratory season.

....

....

....

....

....

SEPTEMBER 29th

In 2004 asteroid 4179 Toutatis passed within four lunar distances of Earth.

....

....

....

....

SEPTEMBER 30th

In 5148 the great Stormcage breakout occurred.

....

....

....

....

OCTOBER 1st

Concorde broke the sound barrier on Earth for the first time in 1969. Thirteen years later another Concorde broke the time barrier and ended up in the year 140 million BC.

....

....

....

....

....

OCTOBER 2nd

Ceremony of the Untempered Schism on Gallifrey.

....

....

....

....

....

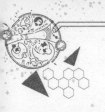

October 3rd

'Save the Drashigs' campaign ended in 3940 after activists were eaten by a Drashig.

....

....

....

....

....

October 4th

The Soviet Union launched Sputnik 1 in 1957, making it the first human-made object to enter space.
The Shadow Proclamation reclassified Earth as a Class 5 civilisation.

....

....

....

....

....

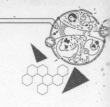

October 5th

The airship R101 crashed on its maiden flight in 1930. It was possibly brought down by Vortisaurs.

October 6th

The Solitract Convergence takes place on this date every 4.2 trillion years.

OCTOBER 7th

Paradox machines were banned under Galactic Federation law in 5246.

....

....

....

....

....

OCTOBER 8th

The banana daiquiri was invented at a party held by Louis XV in 1744 . . .
possibly a few centuries too early.

....

....

....

....

....

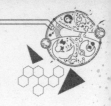

OCTOBER 9th

Ogron Independence Day.

....

....

....

....

....

OCTOBER 10th

Astronomer William Lassell discovered Triton, Neptune's largest moon, in 1846 .
It became the site of a bustling colony before mysteriously falling silent in the thirty-eighth century.

....

....

....

....

....

OCTOBER 11th

In 2011, Agrofuel Research Operations completely changed the way they handled bacteria . . .
especially bacteria with the potential to destroy all plant life.

....

....

....

....

....

OCTOBER 12th

The Mandragora equinox.

....

....

....

....

....

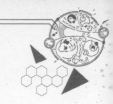

OCTOBER 13th

The Morax spa and beauty salon opened in 2940. Excellent mud baths.
(May be an attempt to infect and take over the bodies of galactic political leaders.)

....

....

....

....

....

OCTOBER 14th

The Battle of Hastings, a pivotal battle that began the Norman Conquest of England, was fought in 1066.
King Harold's Saxons were defeated (despite possession of an atomic canon, later found by Time Agents
at a monastery overlooking the battlefield)..

....

....

....

....

....

OCTOBER **15th**

The first ultra-high-energy cosmic ray was detected on Earth in 1991. It became known as the 'Oh-My-God particle'.

....

....

....

....

....

OCTOBER **16th**

The alignment of the Thirteen Worlds.

....

....

....

....

....

OCTOBER 17th

The Shakri infiltrated Tivoli in 2850 and outmanoeuvred the Vinvocci. They were welcomed as heroes.

....

....

....

....

OCTOBER 18th

Carving Night on Cucurbita. The pumpkin-headed inhabitants of the planet tell stories of monsters that scoop out your brain and leave a candle in its place.

....

....

....

....

October 19th

The Prophesied Wars began in 4000 BC, fought by the mummified warriors of the Foretold.

....

....

....

....

October 20th

In 2820, the cathedrals of the Gothica colony were suddenly filled with people claiming to be from the future . They warned that in one hundred years and two days the entire colony would be overrun with Weeping Angels.

....

....

....

....

October 21st

The Battle of Trafalgar, one of Earth's most famous battles, was fought in 1805 .
Avoid visiting as the battlefield is permanently overcrowded with time travellers.

....

....

....

....

....

October 22nd

The cathedrals of the Gothica colony were overrun with Weeping Angels in 2920.

....

....

....

....

....

OCTOBER 23rd

In 5140, just a week before Halloween, Professor Heiss of Luna University categorically proved that ghosts do not exist. She argued all reports of ghosts have rational explanations, including: Gelth incursions, Cybermen pressing through a dimensional barrier, time travellers stranded in pocket universes, holographic medical AIs and psychic imprints being used as alien transmitters.

....

....

....

....

....

OCTOBER 24th

The magician and escape artist Harry Houdini collapsed on stage in 1926.
He died a week later from unknown causes. Possible alien interference.

....

....

....

....

....

OCTOBER 25th

The flocking of the Quantum Shades.

....

....

....

....

....

OCTOBER 26th

In 2028 the Shadow Proclamation banned the construction of any simulation that
contains virtual people clever enough to work out they are in a simulation.

....

....

....

....

....

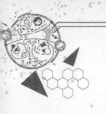

OCTOBER 27th

The Beast of Krop Tor was imprisoned before the dawn of time.

....

....

....

....

....

OCTOBER 28th

The Lupine Wavelength Haemovariforms and the Vulpanans made first contact in 3321.
It was a disaster and marked the start of the Werewolf Wars.

....

....

....

....

....

OCTOBER 29th

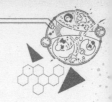

Thassor Orb Launching Ceremony.

....

....

....

....

....

OCTOBER 30th

Orson Welles broadcasted his radio play The War of the Worlds in 1938.
The 'official' report stated many people mistook it for an alien invasion.

....

....

....

....

....

OCTOBER 31st

Halloween. Check that trick-or-treaters are children in costumes — they may be very short alien invaders.

....

....

....

....

NOVEMBER 1st

Krillitane genetic auction. Krillitane from across the galaxy gather to bid on the latest body parts, evolutionary developments and DNA splices.

....

....

....

....

....

November **2nd**

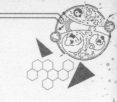

The Morris worm, one of the first computer viruses, was released on to the internet in 1988, causing roughly £5 million in damage. Descendants from its code formed their own civilisation on Digital Sphere H4922 in the twenty-fourth century.

....

....

....

....

....

November **3rd**

Laika the dog became the first mammal launched into space in 1957. Nearby species saw this as evidence that Earth might hold intelligent life, until the first humans followed.

....

....

....

....

....

NOVEMBER 4th

Dr Jane Goodall witnessed chimpanzees creating tools in 1960. It was the first time humans witnessed a non-human animal doing this. Other tool-using Earth animals include crows, octopuses and the renegade sheep of the Great Woolly Rebellion.

....

....

....

....

....

NOVEMBER 5th

Guy Fawkes Night. Humans celebrate a failed attempt to blow up the Houses of Parliament by creating even more explosions. Some aliens believe this tells you everything you need to know about humans.

....

....

....

....

....

November 6th

Ood Sphere Independence Day.

....

....

....

....

....

November 7th

Reaper activity was detected in London in 1987. The lesson for time travellers: avoid paradoxes.

....

....

....

....

....

November 8th

Annual British presidential elections on Parallel Earth.

....

....

....

....

....

November 9th

Spiridon hide-and-seek tournament.

....

....

....

....

....

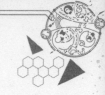

NOVEMBER 10th

Intergalactic Day of Religions That Turned Out to Be an Alien Visitation.

....

....

....

....

....

NOVEMBER 11th

Remembrance Day, Earth and human colonies. Humankind remembers those lost in their many violent conflicts throughout history and promises to try not to do it again.

....

....

....

....

....

NOVEMBER 12th

Tim Berners-Lee published his proposal for a 'WorldWideWeb' in 1990,
a less evil version of WOTAN's plan (see 16 July).

....

....

....

....

NOVEMBER 13th

The colonists of Subterra V retreat below ground in preparation for the acid-rainy season.

....

....

....

....

....

November 14th

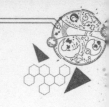

In 2065, after the chaos following the great solar storm of 2064,
self-driving cars are granted citizenship rights.

....

....

....

....

November 15th

After vicious warlord Grand Marshall Skiirgal decided to attach swords to the bottom of his boots,
the Ice Warriors finally invented ice skating on this date in 2950 BC.

....

....

....

....

....

November 16th

The Arecibo radio telescope, located on Earth, broadcasted a message containing basic information about the human race to the globular star cluster Messier 13 in 1974. Messier 13 received the message in 251974.

....

....

....

....

....

November 17th

The Drahvin subjugated Tivoli in 2900 and eradicated the Shakri. They were welcomed as heroes.

....

....

....

....

....

NOVEMBER **18th**

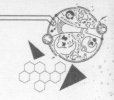

The Pash Pash time of renewal.

....

....

....

....

....

NOVEMBER **19th**

Abraham Lincoln delivered the Gettysburg Address in 1863.
A popular event with time travellers and owners of space–time visualisers.

....

....

....

....

....

November 20th

Soldiers in the Mexican Civil War were abducted by the War Chief in 1910
as part of his attempt to weaponise the human race.

....

....

....

....

....

November 21st

Earth's first colony on Mars, Bowie Base One, activated their nuclear device in 2059 and
completely destroyed the base only seventeen months into the mission. Nobody knows why.

....

....

....

....

....

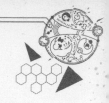

NOVEMBER 22nd

President of the United States John F. Kennedy was assassinated in 1963. Fixed point in time – do not attempt to change. Also, there's already a queue.

....

....

....

....

....

NOVEMBER 23rd

A mysteriously critical date in the space–time continuum. The Nemesis Comet passes close to Earth on this day every twenty-five years. Rival factions of Daleks were witnessed fighting near Coal Hill School in 1963. Humans and Zygons negotiated a peace treaty in 2013.

....

....

....

....

....

November 24th

On Earth, the first amphibious lifeforms experimented with crawling on to land in 410 million BC. It was a Tuesday.

....

....

....

....

....

November 25th

The ghost of Caliburn House was revealed to be future time traveller Hila Tacorien in 1974.

....

....

....

....

....

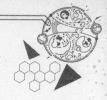

November 26th

Vlad the Impaler, otherwise known as Dracula, conquered the region of Wallachia for the third and final time in 1476. Reports differ on whether he was a vampire, a rogue Saturnyn or a particularly vicious human.

....

....

....

....

....

November 27th

In 2001, the Hubble Space Telescope discovered a hydrogen atmosphere on the planet Osiris, capital of the Osiran Empire.

....

....

....

....

....

November 28th

Earth astronomers Jocelyn Bell Burnell and Antony Hewish discovered the first pulsar in 1967.
They briefly believed it to be an extraterrestrial radio signal.

....

....

....

....

November 29th

The Axos Energy Commission was disbanded in 2670 after accusations of 'space vampirism'.

....

....

....

....

....

November 30th

St Andrew's Day. In 2814, Starship Scotland launched and declared independence from Starship UK.

....

....

....

....

December 1st

Rosa Parks was arrested for refusing to give up her seat on a bus in 1955. She inspired the Montgomery
Bus Boycott and became a hero of the civil rights movement in the United States.
This point in the timestream may be vulnerable to tampering.

....

....

....

....

....

DECEMBER 2nd

In 1993, the space shuttle Endeavour was launched on a mission to repair the Hubble Space Telescope.

....

....

....

....

....

DECEMBER 3rd

London's Metropolitan Police commissioned a new telephone box design in 1929.
The design can be seen in images dating years — even centuries — before.

....

....

....

....

....

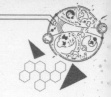

DECEMBER 4th

Winter celebration: the Karn Flame Festival.

....

....

....

....

DECEMBER 5th

The Mary Celeste was found abandoned in 1872. Possible Dalek activity.

....

....

....

....

....

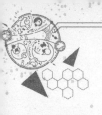

DECEMBER 6th

Winter celebration: Xoanon's Day of Fear on Sevateem.

....

....

....

....

....

DECEMBER 7th

The last Apollo moon mission, Apollo 17, launched in 1972. The mission took the photograph known as The Blue Marble, which showed the human race how small their world was in comparison to the universe.

....

....

....

....

....

DECEMBER 8th

The Hath laid siege to Tivoli in 3001 and chased off the Drahvin. They were welcomed as heroes.

....

....

....

....

DECEMBER 9th

The Kecksburg UFO incident took place in the USA in 1965. Multiple witnesses reported seeing a mysterious fireball in the sky above Michigan and Pennsylvania, while others heard something crash in the woods near Pittsburgh.

....

....

....

....

....

December 10th

The Universal Declaration of Human Rights was adopted by the United Nations in 1948.
It formed the basis for Silurian, alien, clone and robot rights declarations in the following centuries.

....

....

....

....

....

December 11th

Winter celebration: the Feast of Rassilon on Gallifrey.

....

....

....

....

....

December 12th

Winter celebration: Mandatory Celebration Day on Terra Alpha.

....

....

....

....

....

December 13th

Winter celebration: Futurekind Darkworship Time at the end of the universe.

....

....

....

....

....

December 14th

Mystery writer Agatha Christie, who had been missing for eleven days, turned up in Harrogate in 1926 with no memory of what had happened to her. Possible Vespiform presence at this time.

....

....

....

....

....

December 15th

The Great Northern, Piccadilly and Brompton Railway underground line opened in 1906.
This key strategic weakness in metropolitan living would later be exploited by an army of Robot Yetis.

....

....

....

....

....

December 16th

Winter celebration: the Trickster Festival of Might Have Been in the Janus systems.

December 17th

Winter celebration: Neo-Saturnalia in the New Roman Empire during the one-hundred-and-twentieth century.

DECEMBER 18th

The Chula Accords established the human rules concerning time travel in 5130.

....

....

....

....

DECEMBER 19th

The planet Mondas approached Earth in 1986, sparking an attempted invasion by the Cybermen.

....

....

....

....

....

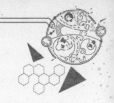

DECEMBER 20th

King Richard I was captured by King Leopold V of Austria after returning from the Crusades in 1192, prolonging the reign of King John and the Cyborg Sheriff of Nottingham.

....

....

....

....

DECEMBER 21st

The Isop and Grem galaxies collided in 350 million BC and formed the Silver Devastation.

....

....

....

....

....

DECEMBER 22nd

Winter celebration: San Claar Divination Day in the Predestined systems.

....

....

....

....

....

DECEMBER 23rd

Winter celebration: the Crystal Feast in Sardicktown and on the planet Ember.

....

....

....

....

....

December 24th

Christmas Eve. Charles Dickens gave a reading in Cardiff in 1869.
Critics praised his dramatic delivery and the impressive special effects.

....

....

....

....

....

....

December 25th

Christmas Day. A time of celebration on Earth and throughout its colonised worlds. Also a time when the planet is
particularly prone to alien invasions. Known invasions include: the Cybermen in 1851, the Great Intelligence in
1892, the Sycorax in 2006, the Racnoss in 2007, the Master in 2009, the Kantrofarri in 2014 and the Shoal of
the Winter Harmony in 2016. A day for family and staying away from major cities.

....

....

....

....

....

DECEMBER 26th

The people of the planet Sto believe humans start boxing on this day.

....

....

....

....

DECEMBER 27th

In 1966 the largest-known cave shaft in the world, the Cave of Swallows,
was discovered in San Luis Potosí, Mexico. Possibly a Silurian base.

....

....

....

....

....

DECEMBER 28th

Winter celebration: the Feast of Traken.

....

....

....

....

....

DECEMBER 29th

The planet Delectilon IV was eaten by a Space Behemoth in 7691.

....

....

....

....

....

DECEMBER 30th

The Great Upload took place in 9000000000. The descendants of the human race uploaded their consciousnesses to the cloud. They downloaded into bipedal meat bodies another 500,000 years later.

....

....

....

....

....

DECEMBER 31st

New Year's Eve. The best New Year's Eve parties to attend include:

Mesopotamia in 3000 BC

Hogmanay in Glasgow in 822

Times Square, Manhattan in 1907

The Chelsea Arts Ball at the Royal Albert Hall London in 1947

Sydney in 1999

Bowie Base Three in 2100

New New York, New Earth, Billennium Celebration, 6000000000

....

....

....